SLEEPING BEAUTY

Cover image: *Sleeping Beauty*, Maxfield Parrish, 1913

The Sleeping Beauty in the Wood (*La Belle au bois dormant*) was first
published in *Histoires ou contes du temps passé*, in 1697.
Monnin's illustrations first appeared in *Contes du temps passé*, 1843.
Gusmand's illustration appeared in *Contes de fées*, 1850.
Doré's illustrations appeared in *Le Contes de Perrault*, 1862.

Doré's illustrations appear on pp. 8, 15, 18, 20, & 21.
Gusmand's illustration appears on p. 37.
All other illustrations are by Monnin.

Sleeping Beauty

Original Text with Classic Illustrations

CHARLES PERRAULT

Translated by
Søren Filipski

Illustrations by
Gustave Doré
E. Monnin

Additional Illustration by
Adolphe Gusmand

Hythloday Press

2014

Sleeping Beauty

The Sleeping Beauty in the Wood

ONCE UPON A TIME, there lived a King and Queen, who were in greater sorrow than words can tell, because they had no children. They traveled to all the rivers of the world, made vows

1

and pilgrimages, and said little prayers. Yet as hard as they tried, nothing worked.

But at last the Queen became pregnant and gave birth to a daughter. They held a beautiful baptism and gathered all the fairies that could be found in the kingdom to give as Godmothers to the little Princess. The King managed to find seven fairies and, following the custom of fairies at the time, he had each one give her a gift. In this way, the Princess was granted all the perfections imaginable.

After the ceremonies of baptism, everyone present returned to the King's castle, where there was a great feast for the fairies. Their table-places were set in magnificent style, each with a solid gold casket containing a spoon, a fork, and a knife of pure gold, all set with diamonds and rubies. But as each was sitting at the table, an old fairy came in who had not been invited. She had not left her tower for fifty years, and people had believed she was dead or under a spell.

The King made her a place at the table, but there was no way to give her a solid gold casket like the others, since only seven had been made—for seven fairies. The old fairy felt insulted, and began to mutter some threats between her teeth.

One of the young fairies happened to hear her and realized that she might give some harmful "gift" to the little Princess. So as soon as they rose from table, she went and hid behind the tapestry, so she could speak last and repair as she could of the damage the old fairy would do.

Soon the fairies began to give their gifts to the Princess. The youngest gave her the gift that she would be the most beautiful person in the world, the second that she should have a mind like an angel, the third that all her actions would be admirable, the fourth that she would dance perfectly, the fifth that she would sing like a nightingale, and the sixth, that she would play every musical instrument to perfection.

When the old fairy's turn came, she shook her head—not because she was old, but out of spite—

and declared that the Princess would prick her hand

on a spindle and die. This terrible gift made the all

the guests tremble, and there was no one who did

not weep.

At that very moment, the young fairy came

out from behind the tapestry, and said these words

aloud:

"Do not worry, King and Queen, that your daughter shall die: it is true that I do not have enough power to undo entirely what my elder has done. The Princess will prick her hand on a spindle; but instead of dying, she shall only fall into a deep sleep that will last one hundred years. In the end, a king's son will awaken her."

The King tried to avoid the misfortune foretold by the old fairy by announcing a law at once, forbidding anyone, on pain of death, from using a spindle or even having one in their home.

One day after fifteen or sixteen years, the King and Queen happened to be out traveling. The young Princess went chasing around the castle, from room to room. When she went up the stairs, she came at last to a small attic at the top of a tower, where a good old woman was sitting alone, spinning with

her spool. This good lady had never heard of the King's ban on spindles.

"What are you doing, my good woman?" said the Princess.

Charles Perrault

"I am spinning, my pretty child," replied the old woman, not knowing who the Princess was.

"My, low lovely!" said the Princess, "How are you doing it? Let me try, so I can see if I can do it just as well!"

Now for one thing, she was hasty, and also very careless, but it was really because of the fairies' decrees that, as soon as she took the spindle, it ran into her hand, and she collapsed.

The frightened old woman cried out for help: people ran up from all parts. They threw water in the Princess's face, unlaced her dress, slapped her with their hands, and rubbed her temples with the Royal Essence of Hungary; but nothing would revive her.

Then the King, who came home when he heard of the commotion, remembered the prophecy of the fairies, and realized that all had happened as the

fairies had said. He put the Princess in the finest apartment of the palace, on a bed of gold and silver embroidery. She was so beautiful that she seemed like an angel. Even her fall had not taken the bright colors from her face. Her cheeks were carnation, and her lips like coral; only her eyes were closed. She could be heard breathing softly, which showed that she was not dead.

The King commanded that she should be allowed to sleep undisturbed until the day of her awakening came.

The good fairy who had saved her life by pronouncing that she would sleep a hundred years was in the kingdom of Matakin, twelve thousand miles away, when the accident happened to the Princess. But she was informed at once by a little dwarf, who had seven-league boots, that is, boots that one could use to travel seen leagues in one stride.

The fairy set out at once, and after an hour people could see her fiery chariot approaching, drawn along by dragons. The King gave her his hand to come down from the chariot. She approved of everything he had done so far, but because she had very great foreknowledge, she also considered the future, when the Princess would finally wake up, and how frightened she would be to wake up alone in this old castle.

So this is what she did: she touched everything in the castle, except for the King and Queen, with her wand—governesses, maids of honor, ladies-in-waiting, gentlemen, officers, stewards, chefs, scullions, runners, guards, porters, pages, footmen. She even touched all the horses in the stables

along with their grooms,
the big mastiffs in the back yard, and
the Princess's little dog Puff, who was with her on
her bed.

No sooner had she touched them than they all fell
asleep, to awaken only at the same time as their mistress, ready to serve her when she needed them. The
very same spits that were ready for the fire, full of par-

tridges and pheasants, fell asleep, and the fire too. All this was done in a moment:—Fairies work quickly.

Then the King and Queen kissed their dear child, without waking her, and went out of the castle. They proclaimed laws forbidding anyone from approaching, but these bans were not needed, because within a quarter of an hour, there grew all around the park a huge number of large and small trees, with brambles and thorns so intertwined into each other, that neither man nor animal could pass through. People could see nothing but the tops of the towers of the castle, and then only from far away. The fairy's magic contrived it this way, so that the Princess had nothing to fear from meddlers while she slept.

Sleeping Beauty

One hundred years later, the son of the King who was ruling then, who came from a different family from the sleeping Princess, happened to go hunting in

that area. He asked what those towers were that he saw over a great thick wood. Each of his companions told him what they had heard. Some said it was an old castle haunted by ghosts; others that all the witches of the country held their rituals there. The most common opinion was that an ogre lived inside, and he carried there all the children he could catch, the better to eat them with ease, since he alone had the power to pass through the wood where no one could follow him.

The Prince did not know what to believe, but an old peasant spoke, and said:

"My Prince, it was more than fifty years ago, but I heard from my father that there was a princess in this castle, the most beautiful in the world; she had to sleep for a hundred years, and would be awakened by the son of a King, for whom she is waiting."

This speech enflamed the young Prince; he decided

at once that since this beautiful adventure had fallen

to him, he would see it through to the end. His desire

for love and glory drove him to set forth at once.

Charles Perrault

But he had barely stepped towards the wood, when all the great trees, the brambles and the thorns, parted on their own to make a passage. He turned forward and entered a long avenue at the end of which he saw the castle. He was a quite surprised when the trees closed behind him as he passed, so that none of his people were able to follow.

Yet he continued his way, for a young prince and lover is always brave.

He entered a large front court, where he beheld a vision that was enough to freeze him with fear: a terrible silence, with the image of death appearing all around. All the collapsed forms of men and animals seemed like lifeless bodies. But when he saw the pimply noses and red faces of the porters, he

knew they were only sleeping; and their cups, which

still held some drops of wine, showed clearly that

they had fallen asleep while drinking. He continued

across a large, marble-paved courtyard, climbed the

stairs, and entered the guardroom. The guards were
standing in their ranks, weapons on their shoulders,

and snoring their loudest. He went through several
rooms full of gentlemen and ladies, all asleep, some
standing, others sitting. At last he entered a room

all covered in gold, and there, lying on a bed, with

the curtains open on all sides, was the most beauti-

ful sight he had ever seen: a princess who appeared

to be fifteen or sixteen years old, and whose radiant

beauty was a thing bright and divine.

He approached, trembling in his wonder, and knelt beside her. At that very moment, the enchantment came to an end, and the Princess awoke. She looked up to him with the tenderest eyes that have ever shone at first sight.

"Is it you, my Prince?" she said, "You're late."

The prince was charmed by these words, and

especially by the way they were spoken, but he did not know how to show his joy and gratitude. He promised her that he loved her more than himself, but his words stumbled out, with much love, but little eloquence. Yet we should not be surprised that he was more embarrassed than she was: she had had time to think about what she would say to him, because—although this is not recorded—the good fairy had given her very pleasant dreams through-out her long sleep. Even after talking for four hours, they had not said half of all they had to tell.

Now the whole palace had awoken with the princess, and everyone returned to their tasks. Yet the servants, because they were not all in love, could feel that they were extremely hungry. The lady-in-waiting, who was as hungry as the rest, grew impatient and finally shouted out loud to the Princess that "Supper is served!"

The Prince helped the Princess to rise; she was fully dressed in a beautiful style, but in an old fashion, with a straight collar like his grandmother. But this did not make her less beautiful, so he didn't mention it.

They went into an apartment full of mirrors, and there ate supper, served by the Princess's stewards. Violins and oboes played old tunes—and played pretty well for being out of practice for a hundred years.

Right after supper the chaplain married them in the chapel of the castle, and the maid of honor took them to bed. Yet they slept very little, since the Princess, after all, had already had enough sleep.

In the morning, the Prince left for his home city and found his father, who had been waiting for him anxiously. The Prince told him this story:

"I got lost hunting in the forest, so I slept in the hut of a charcoal-burner. He fed me black bread and cheese."

The King his father was an honest man and believed him, but his mother was not so easily tricked. When he started to leave almost every day to "hunt," stayed out for two or three nights every time, and always came back with an explanation and an apology, she began to suspect that he was married.

He lived with the Princess for more than two whole years, and had two children. The first was a girl was named Aurora, meaning "Dawn," and the second a son, whom they called "Jour," meaning Day, because he seemed even more beautiful than his sister.

Charles Perrault

The Queen often advised her son to settle down, trying to get him to confide in her. But he never dared reveal his secret. Although he loved his mother, he was afraid of her because she was descended from ogres, and the King had only married her for her money. There was a rumor at the court that she had the appetite of an ogre: when she saw children passing by, she had the hardest time holding back from leaping at them. So the Prince chose not to tell her anything.

But after two years, the King died, and the Prince became the King. At that time, he declared his marriage in public, and traveled with great pomp to his wife the Queen in the castle. She was given a triumphal entry into the capital city, riding between her two children.

A while later, the King went to war against his neighbor, the Emperor Cantalabutte. He left the

Queen his mother to govern the kingdom. Since he was going to be at war throughout the summer, he put his wife and children to her care.

But as soon as he was gone, the Queen Mother sent her daughter-in-law and children to a cottage in the woods, the better to carry out her horrible desires. She went there a few days later and said one evening to her head waiter, "Tomorrow ... for my dinner ... I want to eat ... little Aurora!"

"Oh, Madam!," said the head waiter.

"That is what I want," said the Queen, "and,"—

in the tone of an ogress famished for flesh—
"I would prefer you to serve her with your finest
mustard sauce."

The poor man realized that he could not argue
with an ogress, and went with his big knife to the
room of little Aurora. Now she was only four years
old, and she came to him jumping and laughing, put
her arms around his neck, and asked for candy.

He began to cry, and the knife fell from his
hands. He went into the backyard and slaughtered
a little lamb. He drenched the meat in such a deli-
cious sauce that his mistress swore she had never
eaten so well. Meanwhile, he carried little Aurora
to his wife, and asked her to hide the child in an

apartment at the bottom of the backyard.

Eight days later, the wicked Queen said to her head waiter:

"I want to eat little Jour for my supper."

He gave no answer, planning to trick her as before. He sought out little Jour, and found him with a little foil in his hand, which he was using to fence with a big monkey. (Yet he was only three years old.) He carried the boy to his wife, who hid him with little Aurora. Then he served the ogress a young goat, which was so tender that she thought it was marvelously good.

All went well for a little while after, but one evening the wicked Queen said to the head waiter:

"I want to eat the Queen—with that same sauce as her children."

At that point the waiter lost hope of continuing the trick. The young Queen was twenty years old, not to mention the hundred years she had slept, so her skin was a bit tough, though beautiful and white. There was no way to find an animal that would seem like her.

He decided to save his life in the only way possible, by cutting the throat of the young Queen. He went up to her room, determined to do it once and for all. He worked himself into a fury and entered, dagger in hand, into her bedroom. But he was still reluctant and wanted to hesitate, so he repeated with great care the order he had received from the Queen Mother.

"Do your duty," she said, baring her neck, "Carry out the order you were given. At least then I will see my children again, my poor children whom I loved so much." (She had believed they were dead ever since they had been taken from her secretly.)

"No, no, madam," replied the poor waiter, quite moved. "You shall not die, and you can see your children again, but it will be with me where I hid them, and I shall deceive the Queen by making her a young deer in your place."

He took her promptly to his room, where he left her to kiss her children and weep over them. He went and prepared a young deer. The old Queen ate it for supper with the same relish as if it had been the young Queen.

Feeling well satisfied in her cruelty, she planned that when the King returned, she would claim thatt savage wolves had eaten the Queen his wife and two children. But one evening, as she prowled as usual through the courts and back yards of the Castle to smell out fresh meat, she heard little Jour crying in a cellar, because the Queen his mother wanted to whip for being naughty, and she heard little Aurora begging mercy for her brother.

The ogress recognized the voice of the Queen and her children, and became furious that she had been deceived. The next morning, she ordered, in a terrible voice that made everyone tremble with fright, for a huge vat to be brought in to the middle of the courtyard. It was filled with toads, vipers, snakes and serpents. She planned to throw the Queen and her children into it, along with the waiter, his wife, and her maid. She ordered their hands tied behind their backs.

There they were, with the executioners preparing to throw them in the vat, when the King rode unexpectedly into the courtyard! He came in power, and asked in astonishment what this horrible spec-

tacle meant. No one dared to tell him, but then the ogress, enraged to see what had happened, threw herself headlong into the vat, and was devoured in a moment by the loathsome creatures she had put there.

The King could not help but be grieved, since she was his mother, but it was not long until his beautiful wife and children brought him all the comfort he needed.

Moral

To get a perfect husband takes a wait
That's just the way things are; and you shall find
That virtuous patience is the only bait
To land one handsome, wealthy, brave, and kind.

And what a sweeter pause has ever been?
To sleep a century of peaceful dreams,
And then, to better dreams, awake again!
Such wait is joy, however long it seems.

A long delay brings even greater bliss;
The greatest bliss must suffer long delays.
The god of marriage oaths has promised this:
The love that comes most slowly, longest stays.

   This moral's hard to hear, because it's true.
   To even utter it is hard to do.

Made in the USA
Middletown, DE
02 October 2017